the
cow
loves
cookies

the
cow
loves
cookies

by **karma wilson**

illustrated by
marcellus hall

SCHOLASTIC INC.

ISBN 978-0-545-87397-0

Text copyright © 2010 by Karma Wilson. Illustrations copyright © 2010 by Marcellus Hall.
All rights reserved. Published by Scholastic Inc., 557 Broadway, New York, NY 10012,
by arrangement with Margaret K. McElderry Books, an imprint of
Simon & Schuster Children's Publishing Division.
SCHOLASTIC and associated logos are trademarks and/or registered trademarks of Scholastic Inc.

12 11 10 9 8 7 6 5 4 3 2 1   15 16 17 18 19 20/0

Printed in the U.S.A.   08

This edition first printing, September 2015

Book edited by Emma D. Dryden
Book designed by Debra Sfetsios
The text for this book is set in Coop.
The illustrations for this book are rendered in ink and watercolor.

To Steve Malk, who also loves cookies

and inspired this story. I'd toast you with a glass of milk, but I can't drink the stuff.—K. W.

To Mom and Dad—M. H.

WHENEVER Farmer feeds the horse,

he feeds the horsey **hay,** of course.
The horse just loves to nibble hay.

He eats it
every single day.

But
the
cow
loves
cookies.

Farmer knows
what chickens
need.

He always gives them
chicken feed.

They **scratch** and **cluck** and **peck** all day.

They love their **feed.**

The horse loves **hay.**

But
the
cow
loves
cookies.

The farmer feeds
the geese each
morn.

He always gives
them sweet,
cracked **corn.**

They **honk** for joy and **flap** their wings.

They love the corn that Farmer brings.

Hay for horses,
yes indeed.

Give those chickens
chicken feed.

Corn for geese,
they love it so.

When Farmer
feeds the hogs
their slop,
they love to eat
that gooey glop.

They oink and snort;
they grunt with glee.

They eat like pigs,
it seems to me.

Of course,
we know the horse
loves **hay**.

And chickens love their
feed each day.

Geese love corn,
as all geese should.

The pigs
think slop is
mighty good.

But Cow would never eat that stuff.
You couldn't pay the cow enough!

Because . . .

the
cow
loves
cookies.

Farmer's dog just
loves to eat
when Farmer gives him
doggie treats.

He gulps and gobbles
with delight.

He savors every meaty bite.

Hay is what the horsey needs.

The chickens all
eat **chicken feed.**

The geese munch **corn;**
it tastes so fine.

The hogs think **slop**
is just divine.

The dog adores his
doggy treats.

But Cow would rather
eat things **sweet . . .**

so
why
does
the
cow
love
cookies?

She and Farmer
made a deal,
and every day
they share a meal.

Farmer packs
a picnic lunch,
and when the two
sit down to munch,

he takes
cookies
from a tin

and Cow
gives **milk**
to dunk them in.

Cow is happy.

Farmer too.

They both LOVE milk and cookies!

(But the duck loves quackers.)